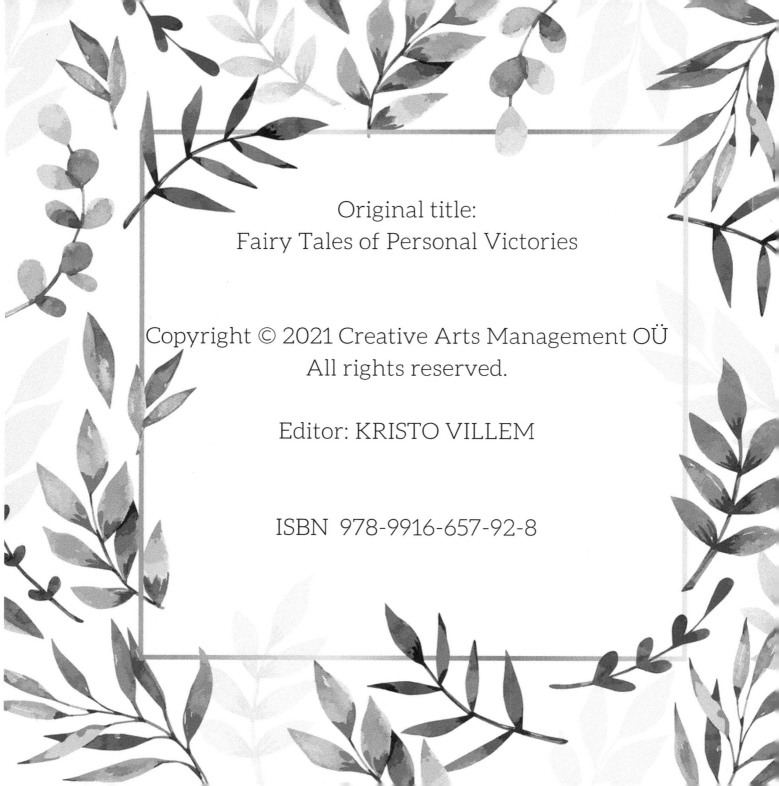

Original title:
Fairy Tales of Personal Victories

Editor: KRISTO VILLEM

ISBN 978-9916-657-92-8

Milo The Sheep

Learn To Trust Life

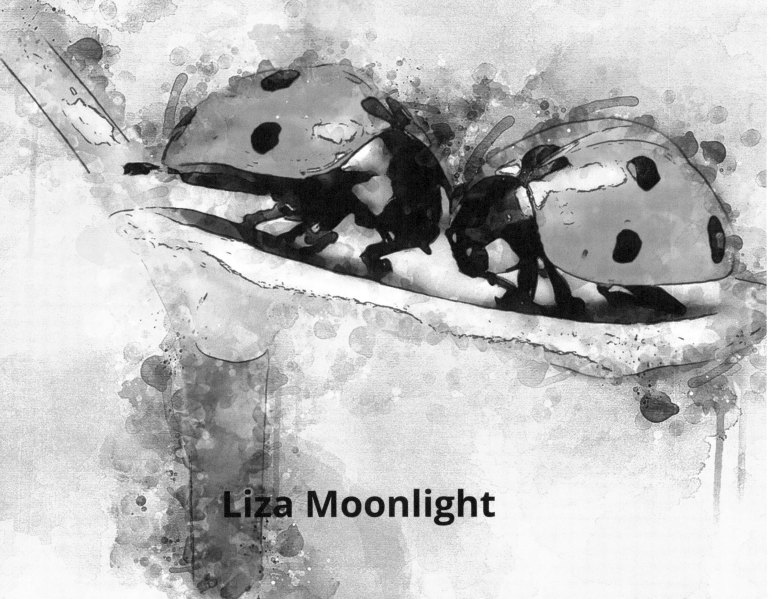

Liza Moonlight

Milo the Sheep was the fluffiest, most cheerful lamb You could possibly imagine. One could even say he was too brave.

He was the most trusting animal in the whole forest and many questioned if he was perhaps too trusting. This unfolding adventure put his trust to the test.

Milo lived by a lake with his mother. One day, however, as Milo woke up, his mother was nowhere to be found. He decided this was the right time to go off and find where mama had gone. The day was sunny and the birds were chirping softly.

The nearby meadows were bewildering. All the beauty of th
nature had blossomed and Milo felt like a newly born little lamb
frollocking around in the soft squishy mud and feeling the warn
sunlight on his wool coat. He knew it's not good to wander off bu
this nature was so very inviting. He ventured further from home.

On the verge of his homely forest, he found an old wooden cabin. A great yellow cat sat by the cabin and Milo asked if the kitty had seen his mother. The cheeky cat looked at this jolly lamb and told him to head south. Milo followed his advice without suspecting anything fishy.

Milo reached the very edge of the forest all to find an old boa
Oh what joy, the lamb thought and hopped on the boat and star
moving upstream toward where the cat had pointed.

owing on the old crooked boat took Milo the rest of the day and
e thought taking a rest would be the best idea. Although Milo still
adn't found a single clue about where his mother might be, he
id not hesitate to travel on as he knew that the trust he had in life
ould eventually carry him to his goals.

He gazed at the sunset and the beauty of this unbelieveab[le]
wonderful natural light show. He felt truly grateful of all the place[s]
he had visited this day. The friendly cat that had guided him to su[ch]
a gorgeous spot and the dreams that he would see soon enough.

new day had dawned and Milo found himself an intriguing path head. A tall strong rocky brick bridge towered above the nature d trees. This would be the best place to look far and wide to nceoover the whereabouts of his mother, Milo thought.

The end of the bridge lead Milo to an abandoned stone hous
Inside the house, he found pieces of wool. So although he did n
see mama from high up, the pieces of wool in this house mu
mean that mama was nearby, right?

nding the pieces of wool gave Milo even more courage and
nthusiasm to go and see more places before eventually finding his
ama. He reached a breathtaking sight - a great big mountain lay
front of him just next to a pond of cooling fresh mountain water.

Well what do you know! Milo was not the only one ready to take
sip from the frest source of water. A pack of wild horses neare
Milo from the distance. It was a hot day so at first, he thought h
eyer were deceiving him. Yet, it was true and the horses we
friendly.

ne horses had heard of a friendly bunny rabbit living in these arts. This rabbit was known for having sharp eyes and seeing all at happens in the forest. Milo took a nice drink from the lake and ecame wery thrilled to find this exciting rabbit.

Milo did not have to look too far, just behind the tall trees was
flickering sight of a carrot. Milo had once again no doubt that th
carrot would belong to the wise little rabbit. Unfortunately, th
bunny had not seen a sheep in these parts but told Milo to kee
looking.

lo was slightly daunted by the fact that even the wise rabbit could
t help him. Slow and steady, he thought and decided to take the
arch from the top. He went to visit the farm where both he and
s mama had grown up. Then, he heard a loud moo and followed it.

The closer Milo got to the familiar sound, the more he remembered journeys from his childhood as him and his mama came to th grassland to visit their family friend Elsid. Elsid and her daught Miru were just beyond a spectacularly crafted old bridge.

d and Miru were grazing in their usual spot, just above a cliff on a autiful flower-filled grassland. Elsid was very glad to see Milo and en she heard of the lamb's trouble, she laughed lightly and asked if had bothered to wait a few minutes before deciding that his mother d gone missing. Perhaps he was behind a tree somewhere.

Now that Milo thought of it, he had never once thought that t
journey would not lead him to his mama. Not a single doubt in
mind, though, how and when he would arrive to his goal, was r
important. He started his jolly trip back towards home.

further he got, the more certain and trustful he got that he will
eet mama as soon as he got home. There was, of course, never a
rtainty that he would find what he was looking for. Trust in life was
that he could muster.

The flowers bloomed brightly as he skipped along the pa[th],
grabbing a bite to eat now and then. he was now close to home a[nd]
so very excited to tell his mama all about his long journey. He kne[w]
his mama was not worried, but rather happy to see Milo.

what a happy moment! Milo found his mother right on the other
e of the home pond. His mama sat quietly just to listen to her
le lamb's stories and marvel at where he had been, She was
nuinely happy for her child's adventures. She knew Milo would
d his way back home and that's what's important,

As the two sheep reunited, the jolly wise rabbit looked from afar a feld glad for them. Milo had learned how to have no expectatic for life. **What we imagine is what we will eventually get, th is the biggest truth in life and the rabbit was happy to ha shared this secret with his new friend.**

Fey the Magical Fairy

Liza Moonlight

Meet Fey. She is known to be one of the most cheerful fairies in the entire world. Fairies are the ones who uphold the light on Earth. However, Fey grew bored of her innate talent and the mission she was given at birth.

u see, all young fairies have a common dream. They dream to
:come a part of human society and see what life is like when
u live among people. This course in a fairie's life always
mes with a risk, however. They might lose their creativity.

To fulfill her life long dream, Fey would need to find a huma
girl who had a similar dream to hers - the child would dream
becoming a fairy. They would then switch places in the tw
worlds, the human world and The Fairyland, where Fey lived.

e sent out her trusty steed, Bella the Unicorn to fetch her
ormation about young human girls who dreamed of
coming fairies. Surely, this must be an easy task, Fey thought,
she bid Bella farewell.

Just as Fey had predicted, it only took Bella a short stroll in th
human world, when she found a little girl in a valley, standir
bare footed with paper mache wings and wishing she could f
just as in her dreams.

ella sent out a signal to Fey and in the blink of an eye, the part
f us which we commonly call the creativity, flew straight from
ey to the little girl. Fey cast a spell towards the girl and in the
ink of an eye, they had switched places in the two worlds.

Fey was just preparing to be transported to the human wor
when a fairy elephant charged on over. He was the
transported along with Fey and they soon woke up in the sun
forest far beyond their home the Fairyland.

oters the Elephant soon became accustomed to the lush
rests of Earth. Both him and Fey took the most of life as the
ain difference between life on Earth and back home was that
eryone had to find their own purpose in life all by themselves.

It was not long before Fey grew bored of the life on Eart
Everything was so plain and simple to her. She summoned
bird to carry her message to Fey's sister. Fey wished to ask he
sister to bring her back home so that she could once aga
send light to planet Earth, albeit from afar.

y's sister, Ariana, received work from Fey as the earthly bird d morphed into a fairy bird to cross the realms. Ariana was ry happy to hear that her sister would return soon. She sent t the word so that everyone would know.

However, Fey's evil step mother would also hear of this new
She had always been jealous of Fey's natural beauty and he
shine. She wanted to stop Fey from returning and to do tha
she would have hide the gateway back to Fairyland.

or the gateway to Fairyland to be hidden, Fey's evil step
other asked her henchman, Erna the Evil Fairy, to dim down
e light in the Magical Lantern. It was the source of light that
one brightly to all who travel between the two worlds.

Erna did as she was told and also hid the lantern away. It ha[s] been kept in the Lantern Cottage for thousands of years. Now however, the mischevous fairy took it to the Great Tower so th[at] noone could possibly reach it.

ey had many friends. Her sister asked the famous hero Elrond
 aid our friend-in-need. The might hero forged a plan to
scue the Lantern from the Great Tower. Elron managed to
treive the Lantern, but something was off, he could just feel it.

Even as the lantern has been brought back from the ominou tower, Fey the lovable fairy was nowhere to be seen. Life passe as ever and some had thought that Fey had deliberate decided to stay behind on Earth.

asons changed and winter followed autumn. Spring followed on after and the summer had bloomed twice. All in good time, ough, Fey fluttered down the snowy mountains of Fairyland to visit her friends and family. This was a big surprise.

Truth be told, Fey knew fair well that she could return to h[er] homeland. The reason for staying behind was that she knew the little girl who had become a fairy in her stead. She enjoye[d] the life in Fairyland so much that Fey did not have the heart [to] bring her back to Earth.

the years had passed, Fey had also learned to enjoy life on
rth. She shared her kindness with everyone and learned to
ve those around her. When the young human girl returned
me to her family, she no longer dreamed of becoming a fairy
t to raise her own family and teach her children about
erything she had learned during her time in Fairyland.

When Fey had reached her own home, just beneath the ch
trees, she felt a rush of creativity. She had not felt it the
time when she lived in Fairyland. This helped her realize th
change in scenery can truly boost our liveliness and teach
how to enjoy life as we do when we are young children. Enjo
life to the fullest is a very important aspect to achieving
goals. Fey knew this well.

ey knew that to live out her full potential in life would mean to
ay connected with herself and know what her true calling in
e is. It is to spread light and love as a fairy and to stay close
ith those who loved her unconditionally.

As you might think, Elrond the mighty hero also liked Fey a l
and as soon as she returned to Fairyland, Elrond asked for h
hand in marriage. Fey, naturally, accepted and so the tw
wonderful fairies got married to live out their lives in the gre
Castle of Imagination. They lived happily ever after.

Hello, friends. Let me tell you the story that happened a long-long time ago in a land called Hiffelpuff. it was a place where everyone enjoyed life to the fullest and were constantly having fun. All the animals and people always laughed and danced. All until one fateful day, that is.

Tiffany the fancy pony had been the guardian of joy in the land of Hiffelpuff. She lived in her castle of Wonders. One starlit night, she went out galloping and once she returned, a tragic thing had happened. Her castle was locked and she had lost her key. This meant she could no longer make potions of joy in her castle. This was a great tragedy indeed.

She called out to her wise old friend, Owly. Owly was well-known for understanding the ways of the stars and she urged Tiffany to look up into the sky to find answers that she so desperately needed. There was not much time until citizens of Hiffelpuff would start to lose their joy.

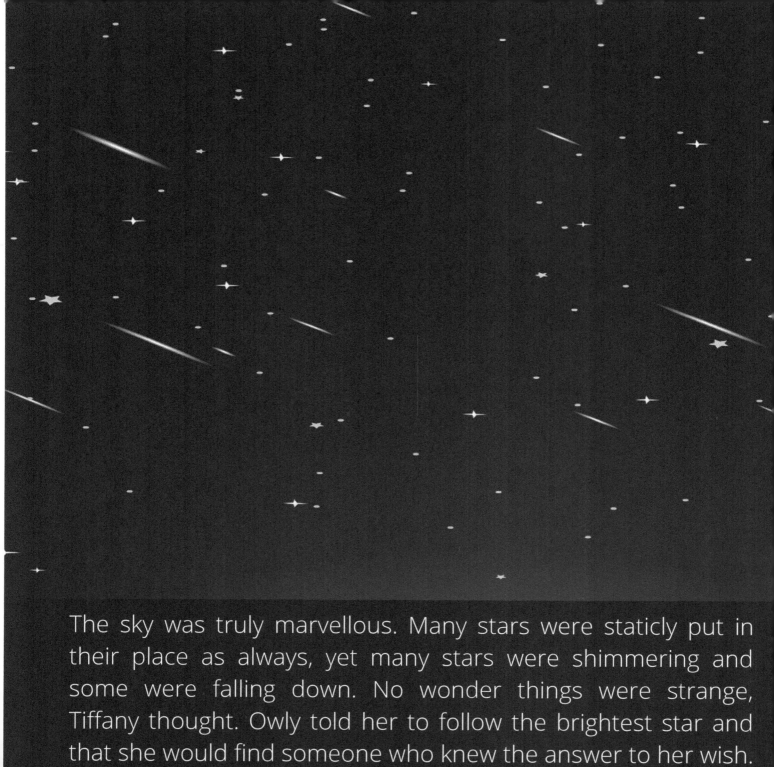

The sky was truly marvellous. Many stars were staticly put in their place as always, yet many stars were shimmering and some were falling down. No wonder things were strange, Tiffany thought. Owly told her to follow the brightest star and that she would find someone who knew the answer to her wish.

The night time was perfect for Tiffany to set sail. She decided the best way to reach the brightest star in the sky would be by boat. The local lighthouse showed a clear path towards the next continent. Tiffany's fish friends came to say goodbye and wish her well. Tiffany the pony was off to solve her big issue.

The first night afloat was a lonely one. Luckily, Tiffany did not have to fear. Sam the Seagull accompanied her little boat all the way to the nearest port. It was much more fun to travel with a firend and they sang each other songs all through the night. What fun it was!

Tiffany reached a great big continent, however, it was arid as a desert. All she could see near the bright red beacon of the sea were two kitties. They encouraged Tiffany to follow her path and said that there was a nice big port at the nearby island of Eldamere. Tiffany was glad to hear friendly words and did not fret.

The further Tiffany sailed, the more friends she made along her way. The Dophin Twins Sif and Saf jumped along eagerly to hear many tales of the pony's travels. Tiffany was more than happy to tell many stories to these newly found fellows. She loved to spend time by telling tall tales of faraway lands.

The first signs of civilized habitat! Hooray! This definitely meant that, eventually, Tiffany would reach a village. hopefully people there will have heard of someone who could help Tiffany. At this point, Tiffany was a very brave soul as she had little to no assurance that this travel would lead to her sought solution.

Finally, Tiffany reached the great port town of Eldamere. The light house keeper kindly offered her a place to rest and sleep .After a good rest and a whole load of hay to eat, Tiffany again set sail. She heard of the wise animals dwelling in the desert of Mayhinder. This was a good place to continue her search.

Tiffany reached the Mayhinder desert with little effort and saw two peculiar animals talking on the hot sand. A tortoise and an armadillo. They had just been discussing that the tortoise had come from a swim at a nearby oasis. What a nice way to spend the hot day, Tiffany thought. The armadillo agreed to see her off.

Tiffany was grateful for the armadillo's service and learned along the way that the wise lion Leander and his family were just about spending time at the oasis. Tiffany seized the opportunity and asked Leander if he knew anyone who could help her retrieve the key she had lost. Leander suggested to visit the wealthiest city on the continent, The Graceland.

It was truly a marvellous city, The Graceland. Tall towers and great merchants were everywhere. Tiffany had never seen such a unique place of prosperity. If there was one place that could be home to people who knew how to find Tiffany's castle key, they would definitely be here, the brave pony thought.

Tiffany met Selda the old witch while galloping around the streets of this city. Selda knew from a single glance at the pony that there was a trouble in this animal's mind. She proposed to craft the pony a new key so that she could once more create potions of joy for the creatures of her home land. For this, she needed fairy spring water, a wooden keg and magical feathers.

Old lady Selda spoke in riddles and told Tiffany to start with the one item she thought was the easiest to obtain. And that the rest would naturally follow. She headed to the local inn and the inn keeper gladly poured the pony some water and said she could keep the keg from which she had been drinking. She heard from the inn keeper that a tournament would be held that day. And that the winner would have their fortune told. Tiffany scurried over, there could be a clue.

Tiffany was the fastest steed of her home land, thus she won the tournament with ease. The winner was announced to the famous magician Hyp. Hyp looked at his infamous crystal ball and said that he would refuse to tell the fortune of Tiffany.

Hyp the Magician said that, instead, he would transport the pony to a mystical place where she would find what she was looking for. This was beyond what the pony had dreamt of, but she was very delighted to accept this proposal.

The moment she had said yes, a very bright color swollowed the pony whole and a tingly feeling suddenly surrounder her. This was a very strange sensation, yet, the pony was trustful and hoped to find what she sought after.

Tiffany reached a land where everything was a turquoise color. Everything except the animals there. They seemed very wise and as Tiffany explained her wish to find fairy spring water, the large elephant stayed silent and without a single word, he motioned Tiffany to follow him.

The elephant of this turquoise land soon joined up with a whole pack of elephants. These great creature travelled the whole night and Tiffany was mesmerized by how persistent they were in their pursuit of fairy spring water. That's what she hoped to find while travelling along with these pure-hearted animals.

Just as she had hoped, in a fortnight, they arrived at the most gallant refreshing springs and pools that Tiffany had ever seen. Mocking birds were drifting atop the glimmering magical water and as Tiffany was in a state of flow, she asked kindly if she could take a feather from the colorful bird's tail. The bird had nothing against it. So, with this, Tiffany had all she needed.

Tiffany quickly rode to the old witch Selda's cabin where she had already invited Ronald to join for this spell. Ronald was the mighties magician in the world and this spell required great skills to cast. After the incantation was complete, a shiny golden key fell from the sky. It was just like the one Tiffany had had before and she was very happy to be able to return home. Her home village was now saved. everyone could dance and sing once more!

Truth be told, the happy ending was indeed happy. However, it was Selda's daughter, Helda the wise young witch who dropped the key from the sky. You see, the components for the spell were unnecessary. Sometimes, we face tests to see if we really mean what we say and do, if we are worthy of what we are looking for. And to prove our worth, we need to persevere. That is exactly what Tiffany did. She stayed true to her mission and was rewarded kindly. If you wish for something in Your life, my friends, the Key is to never give up! YOU WILL WIN! See you next time!

STORIES THROUGH SEASONS

LIZA MOONLIGHT

Greetings, friends! This story will teach you the ever changing flow of time. As time passes, so do the seasons. There are many lovely things to each season and each of them holds many secrets and surprises.

Enjoy these tales and hopefully you will also discover something new!

Everything that surrounds us has patterns. As the day always follows the night and the sun always sets and then rises, the seasons also follow one another. The first season of our book's cycle is Spring. It a time of many new beginnings. Birds return to their homeplaces and the sun start to give more and more warmth. Chippy the Bird will be Your guide!

It is probably no surprise that the thrilly easter rabbit family comes out to enjoy the sun and play around on the warm grass. They have been sitting snugly in their burrows for the whole winter and are so very happy to be outside and hop around and flop their ears.

As the first leaves are turning green, the birds find their favourite spots to to make their nests. Spring is the perfect time to hatch eggs so that bird babies can learn how to fly and explore their own lives.

The cherry trees blossomed and bloomed as white as snow. A cute fat yellow bird flew onto the tree to smell the sweet scent and feel the soft breeze high up on the tallest branch. This made the birdy flap his wings gently.

Candy the young kitten was so relieved that the whole countryside had turned green. She purred and rolled around enthusiastically. She found a tiny lake and bravely went on to have a quick swim in the warm water.

Hoppy the floppy-eared brown rabbit was eagerly waiting for the seeds to start sprouting first leaves out of the earth. She could not wait until the sweet-sweet carrots are finished and she could sink her sharp teeth into them, filling her belly with delicious carrot juice.

As Chippy had been looking at all of these wonderful animals, the Spring had gradually turned to Summer. The weather was now much warmer and everything was in full bloom. Chippy went on to see what kind of adventures the animals of the forest had undertaken. So exciting!

The kitten twins, Mew and Mow had been playing around on an open field when their pal, Roofers the hound dog found them to give them a paw with cleaning up their fur coats. They were newly born kittens and their splendid white coats had gotten dirty from all the rolling and jumping. Roofers was glad to help them out.

The summery days were filled with laughter and games. A tiny mouse spurried across the great open plains, chasing a huge butterfly. This butterfly was multiple times larger than the mouse was, even so the mouse was not afraid to chase after the big bug. It was great fun.

Very near to where the mouse had been playing there were Mr. Zebra and Mrs. Giraffe. They were casually chatting along and discussing the wonderful warm weather. Both of them could graze to their hearts' content. Neither of them had a single worry.

Naturally, no summer is complete without strawberries. Two little colorful butterflied woke up this morning to go out and do a scavenger hunt. The most difficult part was to find the most scrumptious strawberries and that was exactly what they found right next to a lake with the most stunning view. They were both very pleased.

On such a fine day as this, all of the kittens want to run around and play as much as they possibly can. This playful little cat found a colorful ball that was even bigger than himself. This did of course not bother him and he decided to play and have a lot fo fun. The ball was filled with air.

Time passes and along with it, everything and everyone changes too. Chippy's feathers have turned brown as the falling leaves and the impending Fall is just around the corner. Now the days grow shorter and the nights grow colder. Even so, Chippy knows this is not a bad thing, it is just how nature is, was and always will be.

The occasional rain is a welcomed part of Fall. the more rain that pours down the more the late harvest gets to fluorish. Clouds gather and disperse. The strong gusts of wind will eventually shake away the clouds and the rain will have to stop. Sometimes soon, possibly.

Just as the rain had stopped, the two friendly puppies, Spark and Woofa came out of their dog houses to marvel at how the nature had started to show its colors thanks to the abundant water. The usually calm river that flows past their houses was flowing with great speed and they were barking happily as the cool water flowed past them.

If there was one animal who really knew how to enjoy any kind of weather then it was Candy the kitten. She sat in the warm springy yellowish grass, looking at the birds flying past to the South. She liked how the wind was still warm as she yawned calmly, listening to the waterfall right next to where she had been sitting. Such a relaxing sound.

Mr. Zebra and Mrs. Giraffe were still talking, even now. They were discussing how lovely the colorful trees looked. So vibrant. So many colours. Both of them were very keen to find out what kind of a Winter there would be this year. It cannot be long now, they thought. The days were now quite chilly.

Felix the Fox was still a very young fox cub. He did not quite understand why the leaves of all the trees had started to fall off. His mother told him to wait patiently as in time all the questions will be answered.

Chippy was wise to know that the more he flew about, the more warm he would be. Birds do not have to worry about the cold so long as they keep moving. The Winter had come. A nice friendly kid had made a snowman right next to Chippy's favourite fence and he added a carrot for the funky looking snowman so that it would be complete.

One thing that all of the animals of this forest always looked forward to was that in the winter time, the night sky would oftern light up in very beautiful colours. All the animals would gather around to see this spectacle. It was something they would only see in Winter.

You have probably heard of the mighty Mammoths. This mammoth was angry at how the tiny people always stepped on his tail. He thought they would all see the furry creature's tail but was so fluffy that it wiggled and wagged around in the wintery breeze. This human wearing a red hat bumped into the mammoth and there was nothing he could do . He was simply that big.

Even though Emma the wolf mother knew well that howling might frighten other citizens of the forest, she could not help herself when she saw the full moon of the December sky. It excited her to be able to send out word to all of the other animals to look up into the sky. Not many look at the sky at all, don't you agree?

When morning arrived, Emma was still howling. She had gotten too excited and had trouble pulling the breaks. Luckily the old wise moose Manfred was just walking past Emma and suggested that she dug her nose in the cold snow. She tried it and the cold snow helped her calm down.

Our story of the Seasons has come to an end but before we call it a close, leave it to Chippy to bring you the moral of this story. Bear this is in mind:

Everything in your life is in ever lasting change. Nothing you know will always stay the same. It is important to accent that letting go is something we must learn and the more we let go of the old, the more room will be born. Even if the future is sometimes scary. Stay healthy!

Thank You for reading This Book!

To show our **appreciation**,
here is a
FREE additional **Story**!

Download at:

CPSIA information can be obtained
at www.ICGtesting.com
Printed in the USA
BVHW021404240521
608002BV00011B/1967